T0123388

WHAT IN THE WORLD IS GOING TO HAPPEN

DENNIS MATHER

WESTBOW
PRESS®
A DIVISION OF THOMAS NELSON
& ZONDERVAN

Scripture taken from the New King James Version®. Copyright © 1982
by Thomas Nelson. Used by permission. All rights reserved.

WestBow Press books may be ordered through booksellers or by contacting:

WestBow Press
A Division of Thomas Nelson & Zondervan
1663 Liberty Drive
Bloomington, IN 47403
www.westbowpress.com
1 (866) 928-1240

ISBN: 978-1-5127-4558-0 (sc)
ISBN: 978-1-5127-4559-7 (e)

Library of Congress Control Number: 2016909467

Print information available on the last page.

WestBow Press rev. date: 7/15/2016

He causes all, both small and great, rich and poor, free and slave, to receive a mark on their right hand or on their foreheads.
—Revelation 13:16

WHAT IN THE WORLD
IS GOING TO HAPPEN?

"Where are Auntie and Katy?" Amanda asked from the back seat.

"I don't know!" was all I could muster.

I'm Susan. My sister, Sally, and I, along with my thirteen-year-old daughter, Amanda, and Sally's thirteen-year-old daughter, Katy, were driving to the mall this morning. All of a sudden, I realized Sally was not answering me. I looked over to the passenger side, and she was not there.

That was when Amanda asked her question.

We were only three miles away from Rodger and Sally's farm, so I turned back. Rodger, along with two of their kids, Brad and Tim, were home that morning when we left, because it was summer vacation.

Brad, Rodger and Sally's seventeen-year-old, met us at the door. "Dad and Tim vanished all of a sudden, and I can't find them anywhere!" he exclaimed.

"Your mother and Katy are gone too!" I blurted out.

"I'll bet this is the rapture they were always talking about," Brad cried.

"Oh, I hope not!"

Then my cell phone rang. It was my husband, Jason. "Are you okay?" he asked. "There are three people here at work that we can't find!"

"Yes, I know! Sally, Rodger, Timmy, and Katy are missing too. But Brad is here!"

"I'll bet this is the rapture they were always talking about!" Jason exclaimed. "Is Amanda all right?"

"Yes, she is here with me. Brad thinks it's the rapture too!"

"I'm coming home right away!"

"Okay, I'll see you there."

"Timmy and Katy were always getting in trouble in class for speaking out about the Bible," said Brad. "I wish I'd heeded their pleas for accepting Jesus Christ when I had the chance!"

It was well-known that Brad was a rebel. He hadn't gone to church with the family for about a year and was always going to parties with the rest of the football team.

Jason got home a few minutes after I did. "Bradley called and said he wanted us to come out because he wanted to talk about what had happened today," I explained.

It was only seven miles out in the country, so we called him back and responded, "Okay!"

After eating some pizza, we went out to Rodger and Sally's farm.

"I've discovered that Dad has been doing a lot of writing lately," said Brad. "I was convicted just now from reading his writings and accepted Jesus Christ! I can now understand what the Bible says about prophecy and what my family was saying all along. I truly believe it was the rapture that happened today."

"You know, I believe it was the rapture too," Jason replied. "Should I accept Jesus Christ in order to know what is going to happen next?"

"Yes! That would be a good idea," answered Brad.

"Okay, I'm in. What do I do?"

"Just say, 'Lord Jesus, I'm a sinner and need what You did on the cross to forgive me of my sins. Come into my life, and make me whole!'"

Jason prayed that prayer, and I prayed about five minutes later, after Jason stopped praising the Lord. We had to persuade Amanda for about ten minutes, but she finally accepted Jesus, and all four of us were praising the Lord.

"Do you want to see what Dad has been writing?" asked Brad.

"Okay, let's see what he has been doing!"

"Yes, let's have a Bible study," Amanda and I said in unison.

"Okay, I'll go get some of it. There is a lot, so we can't get through it all tonight."

Brad came back and presented it to us.

The Doctrine of Last Things

The doctrine of last things is known as eschatology, which is the study of certain events of the last days. It is the Greek words *eschatos* and *ology* put together. Eschatos means "latter end"[1] and speaks of those things that will be happening at the end of, or directly after, our present dispensation.[2] And of course, *ology* means "science" in Greek.

We do not know exactly when these events will take place, because "it is not for [us] to know" (Acts 1:7). However, we can know the general timeframe (Luke 21:29–31). And one of the best ways of knowing this is the fact that Israel is being regathered, which takes place in the last days (Ezekiel 36:24-38; 37:1-28; Zephaniah 3:14–20; Zechariah 10:8–11; Romans 9:15–16). She is also getting herself ready for that which God has in store for her, which is having her Messiah sitting

---

[1] James Strong, *The Exhaustive Concordance of the Bible* (New York and Nashville: Abingdon Press, 1970), item #2078 in the Greek dictionary.

[2] A dispensation is a dispensing of God's grace that takes place in a time period. This grace is different in each period, so that what constituted a salvation plan in the previous dispensation is invalid in the present dispensation. This is due to progressive revelation. For instance, the Patriarch dispensation didn't have the Ten Commandments, and the Mosaic dispensation didn't have the Immanuel coming of Jesus Christ. There have been six dispensations put into effect since the fall of humanity. They are conscience, human government, patriarch, Mosaic, kingship, and church. The millennium, which is the seventh dispensation, is still in the future.

on David's throne in Jerusalem, even though Israel is now in a state of unbelief.

On top of all this, the "gathering around Jerusalem for battle" (Zechariah 14:2; Revelation 16:16, 19:19) that is spoken of in the Bible is beginning because of the hatred of many people for the Jewish state, especially those in her immediate vicinity.

We will examine this phenomenon and seven other things in this treatise. They are the following:

1) the apostasy,
2) the rapture,
3) the tribulation period,
4) the glorious second coming of Jesus Christ,
5) the resurrections and judgments,
6) the millennium, and
7) the new heaven and new earth.

1) The Apostasy

The apostasy is where we are living right now and is based upon the fact that "the mystery of iniquity is already at work" (2 Thessalonians 2:7). The stage is being set up for those things that are going to happen after our present dispensation ends. So it is good to know what is going on in our present day.

Many things are included in this apostasy. First, people are now in a condition that is commensurate with that which is depicted in 2 Timothy 3:1–7. Second, there is an increase of knowledge in the latter days, as predicted by Daniel in Daniel 12:4. And third, the world can think of only one thing, and that is the quest to become a one-world society.

It can also be seen by these facts that we are in the last days just prior to the rapture (Matthew 24:32–33, 37; 2 Thessalonians 2:7–8).

2) The Rapture

The rapture is when born-again Christians of all nations will be delivered from "the wrath to come" (1 Thessalonians 1:10; Revelation 3:10). It is the event that will end the church dispensation and is the next event in eschatological history.

It is accomplished by our being caught up in the clouds to be with Jesus Christ (1 Corinthians 15:51–54; 1 Thessalonians 4:14–18) and is certainly our "blessed hope" (Titus 2:13). It is also why everyone who is born again is at the "marriage" and the "marriage supper" of the Lamb in heaven (2 Corinthians 5:8; Revelation 19:7, 9), while everyone who did not participate in it is left on earth to go through the tribulation.

3) The Tribulation

The tribulation is that period of time between the rapture and the glorious second coming of Jesus Christ. It takes place on earth while born-again believers are in heaven.[3] It has also been known as Daniel's seventieth

---

[3] We are in heaven only for a short time, because Revelation 19:14 says we will come back with Jesus when He returns. We go to heaven to sleep when we die (1 Thessalonians. 4.14–15; Song of Solomon 5:2a). And when we awake, we are to have a great banquet (Revelation 19:7–9) before we saddle up on white horses behind Him. Those who are raptured go to the banquet without sleeping.

week (Daniel 9:24–27),[4] the time of "Jacob's trouble" (Jeremiah 30:4–9), and "the hour of temptation" for the Gentiles (Revelation 3:10).

The tribulation period is seven years in length and has two halves, each 3.5 years long (Daniel 9:27). The first half sees the regimes of the Antichrist and the false prophet come into being,[5] and only during this time in history will the world see these two in power (2 Thessalonians 2:7–8; Revelation 6:2–11). The second half is very cataclysmic and is the judgment of the Gentiles (2 Thessalonians 2:9–12; Revelation 6:12–17).

Israel has somewhat peaceful conditions in the first half of the tribulation because it has entered a peace pact with the Antichrist (Daniel 11:21–23; Isaiah 28:14–18) through the help of the false prophet (Revelation 13:12; Zechariah 11:16–17; Revelation 18:3). But even this treaty does not ensure a lasting peace for Israel, because at the halfway mark of the tribulation, the Antichrist and the false prophet desecrate the temple that has been built in Jerusalem (Daniel 11:31; Matthew 24:15). This is when Israel flees to a safe place (Matthew 24:16–20; Mark 13:14–20; Luke 21:20–21; Revelation 12:6,

---

[4]   Daniel's seventieth week is based upon the fact that the weeks in Daniel 9:24–27 are seven-year periods. It also includes the fact that the church dispensation is a parenthesis inside the kingship dispensation between the sixty-ninth and seventieth weeks. This is so the Gentiles can come to know the Messiah and is portrayed for us in Romans 9:24–11:15.

[5]   The Antichrist will someday be the dictator of the world (Revelation 13:1–10; Daniel 11:21–45; Revelation 17:7–8, 11), and the false prophet will someday be the leader of the "one world church" (Revelation 13:11–18; 17:1b–6, 9, 18; 18:2–24).

14–16) that has been prepared for her in the countries of Edom, Moab, and Ammon (Daniel 11:41; Revelation 12:16a).[6]

The second half of the tribulation is when our Lord judges the earth. Much is said in the Bible about this (Zechariah 14:1–6; Rev. 6:12–17, 8:7–21, 14:18–20, 16:1–21, 19:17–21), because God does not wish that anybody should have to go through it (2 Peter 3:9). The first half of the tribulation may bring wars, famines, diseases, and a dictator (Revelation 6:1–9), but the second half will bring cataclysmic devastation that people have never seen before (Revelation 6:12–17). That this period of time is very short is indicative of the fact that God is merciful (Matthew 24:22; Mark 13:19–20).

4) The Glorious Return of Jesus Christ

The glorious return of Jesus Christ is also known as the second coming because it is the second time

---

[6]   In *The Wycliffe Bible Commentary,* (The Moody Bible Institute, 1962), Wilbur Smith says while commenting on Revelation 12:13–17 that "the earth's aiding the woman (v. 16) may represent, as Walter Scott says, the governments of the earth befriending the Jew 'and providentially (how, we know not) frustrating the efforts of the serpent.'" So the countries south and east of Israel where Saudi Arabia is now located (Edom, Moab, and Ammon) are ancient Arabic countries that were in the general area that is now the country of Saudi Arabia. They will again aid Israel in the future when she is under persecution. They did this unknowingly in 1991 during the Persian Gulf War when it was thought that the leader of Iraq, Saddam Hussein, sought to destroy Israel. Saudi Arabia hosted the armies that ousted Saddam.

He will actually put His feet on the ground.[7] It occurs at the end of the tribulation period and is for the purpose of curtailing the activities of both the Antichrist and the false prophet who will have gathered the entire world together for battle against Israel.

Jesus will come quickly, as He said He would (Revelation 3:11; 22:7, 12, 20), and the Antichrist and false prophet are put directly into "a lake of fire burning with brimstone" (Revelation 19:20).

Everyone else who is present at this pseudo battle known as Armageddon is "slain with the sword of Him that sat upon the horse, which sword proceeded out of His mouth" (Revelation 19:21). And this person sitting on the horse is Jesus Christ at His second coming.

5) The Resurrections and Judgments

There are three resurrections in the future that are all in conjunction with three judgments. They are one that pertains to born-again Christians, one that pertains to righteous Old Testament saints, and one that is for the unsaved of all ages.

---

[7] At the rapture, Jesus will catch us in the clouds (1 Thessalonians 4:17), but at the second coming, He will come down through the clouds and put His feet on the ground (Matthew 24:30, 26:64; Daniel 7:13; Luke 21:27; Mark 13:26, 14:62). Putting His feet on the ground constitutes an advent.

A. The Resurrection and Judgment for Christians

The resurrection we are speaking of for Christians is the rapture (1 Thessalonians 4:17), and the judgment is the "Judgment Seat of Christ" (2 Corinthians 5:10).

The judgment seat of Christ is also called "the bema seat," the place where the Greek participants of the Olympics went to get their rewards. So also we go to this judgment not to receive condemnation (Romans 8:1), but to receive our rewards for a job that is "well done" (Matthew 25:21). This does include, however, the fact that we might experience the loss of rewards that we could have had if we would have lived lives that were more in accordance with God's will for us (1 Corinthians 3:9–15; Romans 14:10–13).

B. The Resurrection and Judgment for Righteous Old Testament Saints

There is a judgment in conjunction with the resurrection that is found in Daniel 12:1c–3. It is also not for the purpose of condemnation, because these are saved people. But it is for the purpose of giving rewards to everyone who died righteously from the first through fifth dispensations. This is so they will be ready for the millennium.

In addition, this resurrection and judgment is also for those who will be saved during the tribulation period.[8] This is why it will take place after the tribulation and before the millennium starts.

C. *The Resurrection and Judgment for the Unsaved of All Ages*

The judgment that the unsaved of all ages encounter is called "the great white throne judgment" (Revelation 20:11–13) and is also known as the "second death" (Revelation 20:5–6). It is also when everybody who has not accepted Jesus Christ as his or her personal Savior throughout all of the dispensations is put into the "lake of fire" for all of eternity (Revelation 20:14–15, 22:11). [9] It takes place after the millennium and before the new heaven and new earth are created.

6) The Millennium

The millennium is the thousand-year period that will take place after the tribulation period and before the new heaven and new earth are created. It is when Jesus Christ will reign in person on King David's

---

[8] Many scholars believe that Ephesians 4:8–10 speaks of when Jesus Christ went to "Abraham's bosom" (Luke 16:22) and brought its inhabitants to heaven to be with Him. I believe this is true, which is why these people will be at this judgment. As has been noted, those individuals who are saved during the tribulation period will also be at this judgment. They are the 144,000 Israelites who are sealed by the Lord in Revelation 7:3–8, the Gentiles mentioned in Revelation 7:9–14, and a remnant of Israelites who are found in Revelation 12:6; Zechariah 14:2, 5, and Ezekiel 14:21–23.

[9] Luke 16:23–24 indicates that people who are in Hades have some sort of a body, and they have these bodies so they will be able to stand judgment.

throne in Jerusalem (2 Samuel 7:4–17; 1 Chronicles 17:4–15; Psalm 89:3–4; Revelation 19:16) with "born-again Christians" at His side on the thrones that He has promised to them (1 Corinthians 6:2; Revelation 5:10, 20:4).[10] The millennium is found in Psalm 72:7–17; Isaiah 2:2–4; Micah 4:1–7; Zechariah 14:16–19; Isaiah 24:23, 35:1–10; Jeremiah 23:5–8; Isaiah 65:19–25; and Revelation 20:3–10.

Everyone who will be saved during the tribulation, as well as those who will be present at the Daniel 12:1c–3 resurrection, will go into the millennium to start the nations once again. Jewish people, of course, will start the nation of Israel (Ezekiel 34:11–31), and Gentiles will start the other nations (Zechariah 14:16; Revelation 20:8).

There will be only a partial lifting of the Genesis curse during the millennium, because death will still be present (Isaiah 65:2). This is why I believe that people who are living on earth during the millennium will do so in a resurrection body that was like Jesus' resurrection body (Luke 24:39–43).

However, the resurrection body is not the final body that everyone will inhabit. At the creation of the new heaven and new earth, everyone who has not perished in judgment will inherit another perfect body that we will call "a glorified spiritual body" (1 John 3:2; 1 Corinthians 15:42–44; Philippians 3:21).

---

[10] Second Corinthians 5:8 and 1 Thessalonians 4:17 say that either after death or after the rapture, Christians will be in the Lord's presence (see footnote 3). This is when we will begin to reign with Him (Revelation 5:10). This is also why I think we live in a "palace" on earth during the millennium (Song of Solomon 1:4c, 12).

There will be an apostasy at the end of the millennium when Satan will be released for a little while (Revelation 20:7–9). This release is for the purpose of testing those individuals who will be born during this time but only have a nominal profession and allegiance to our Lord. In other words, they will not be born again to a heart belief in Jesus Christ. He will give them the chance to live for Him, but in their hearts, they will not really accept Him as Lord (Matthew 7:21).

Needless to say, fire will come down from heaven and devour all those who participate in this rebellion (Revelation 20:9c), so these individuals will be found at the great white throne judgment.

7) The Final State

Eternity future is when a new heaven and new earth will be created (Revelation 21:1) and is when all the curses, including the curse of death, will finally and for all time be done away with (Revelation 21:4, 27).

The final state will come after the millennium is completed and after our present heaven and earth are destroyed (2 Peter 3:10–12). It will also demonstrate the way things will be for all of eternity (Revelation 22:11).

* * *

"Wow!" Jason exclaimed.

"Yes, wow!" I echoed.

"Super wow!" shouted Amanda. "I can see that the Lord has really been giving him the scoop."

"I have to go to work in the morning, and it's been a big day, so I guess we'd better vamoose. Thanks for having the Bible study tonight!" said Jason.

"Yes, and I'm kind of tired, too," I responded. "Thanks, Brad, for showing us Rodger's writings.

"Yes, thanks!" exclaimed Amanda.

"You're all welcome. Maybe we should get together tomorrow because there's more. I didn't realize he was doing so much writing."

"Are you going to be all right here by yourself?" asked Jason.

"Yes, Dad and I were fixing the fence in the spare pasture so we could put the cows in where the grass is high. They have eaten the one they're in way down.

So I'll work on that; it's almost finished. But come out tomorrow because there are more of Dad's writings to study!"

"I'll call to see how you are doing on the fence before we come," Jason promised.

"Okay, see you tomorrow!" we all said.

Amanda and I listened to and watched the news the next day and found what was happening in the world very interesting. Jason had gone out to the farm to help Brad finish the fence.

Just to get us all caught up, Boano Schmidt, the Chancellor of greater Germany (which was the old European Common Market and ten different 'super powers' joined together) had a news conference where he said he was establishing Germany's total control over the world. He also said he was giving the leaders of the ten previously mentioned 'super powers' more power, so the world would function more efficiently.

He set a very strong leader over each of these areas who would answer to him. However, each of these leaders would have full control over their area.

He also named this new world order One World Community. He said he was the supreme political leader of this one-world community, and that he and it were the end of the law that should be obeyed unequivocally.

He also said he was leaving for the Vatican right after the news conference to confer with his good friend, Pope St. Boniface. This man brought the Roman Catholic Church into the World Council of Churches about five years prior. That body is an ecumenical body of most of the churches of the world. St. Boniface declared then that he was the leader of this new World Council of Churches. The evangelical churches of Christ, along with most Pentecostal denominations, had already joined up.

At about the same time, St. Boniface joined the Khomeini of Iran and the leader of Egypt to his organization. (These two are the king of the north and the king of the south in Daniel, chapter eleven, and were the leaders of the Islamic world.) St. Boniface also joined the patriarch leaders of the Orthodox and Russian churches in Eastern Europe to the fray.

When they did this, they developed a center of world religions in Rome. Eastern religions such as Hinduism and Buddhism, along with cultic, atheistic, and animistic religions, also had this organization in Rome as their headquarters. St. Boniface said by satellite at the news conference today that he was the supreme leader of all that is spiritual in the world.

Amanda and I also studied and looked up biblical references all day in the material Rodger had written that we brought home. We were looking forward to going to the farm to see what else Rodger had written.

I took a string bean casserole and some Maid-Right that I cooked with us, because I knew Brad and Jason had been fencing all day and were probably pretty tired and hungry.

When we arrived, we prayed and gave thanks for the food.

"*Mmm,* this is good!" Brad said when he began wolfing down the food I had brought.

When we finished, we prayed again, and then Brad brought out some more of Rodger's writings. They were seen to be as follows.

1) The Two Beasts of the Tribulation Period

Two individuals are explained in Revelation, chapter thirteen, and are depicted as separate beasts. One is a beast that rises "up out of the sea" (13:1), and the other comes "up out of the earth" (13:11). A significant thing that can be seen when studying the texts pertaining to these two beasts is that the beast coming out of the sea has ten horns, and the beast coming out of the earth has two horns.

A. The Beast that Comes Out of the Sea with Ten Horns

The first beast mentioned in Revelation 13 comes out of the sea and has ten horns. That this beast comes out of the sea is significant, because it portrays the "sea of nations." As John F. Walvoord has written, "The fact that the beast rises out of the sea is taken by many to indicate that he comes from the great mass of humanity, namely the Gentile powers of the world."[11]

Merrill Unger, while commenting on Revelation 13, said about this beast,

> "The beast [has a] wicked career, [verses] 6–10. He blasphemes God and those who are His, (6). To this end he wars against the saints, (7a)

---

[11]   John F. Walvoord, *The Revelation of Jesus Christ: A Commentary by John F. Walvoord* (Chicago: Moody Press, 1974), 198.

(Daniel 7:21–22; Revelation 11:7, 12). He is permitted unrestrained power over all earth dwellers except over the elect, (8–10) (c.f. Matthew. 24:13, 22). He is the antichrist, the man of sin (2 Thessalonians 2:3–12; 1 John 2:22, 4:3)."[12]

As we will see as we go along, the book of Daniel is a parallel book to the book of Revelation. So this beast is also found in Daniel 11:36–39, where he is militarily inclined, among other things.

The horns of this beast are ten kings that give their power to the beast (Revelation 17:12). This beast is the Antichrist, who has the whole world in his grip (Revelation 13:3–4).

B. The Beast that Comes Out of the Earth with Two Horns

The second beast in Revelation 13 has two horns and comes out of the earth. The phrase "from the earth" depicts that false religion, from ancient times to the present, has always "worshipped and served the creature rather than the Creator" (Romans 1:25), so it is actually the earth and all that is in it that is being worshipped. Hence, this beast comes "up out of the earth."

Walvoord writes,

The reference to the second beast as coming out of the earth indicates that this character, who is later described as

---

[12] Merrill F. Unger, *Unger's Bible Handbook* (Chicago: Moody Press, 1967), 863.

> a false prophet (Revelation 19:20), is a
> creature of earth rather than heaven …
> He is pictured [here] as having two horns
> like a lamb and as speaking like a
> dragon. The description of him as a lamb
> seems to indicate that he has a religious
> character, a conclusion supported by his
> being named a prophet. His speaking as
> a dragon indicates that he is motivated by
> the power of Satan who is "the dragon."[13]

This second beast also causes the whole earth to worship the first beast by doing miraculous things (Revelation 13:12–15). [14] This being the case, he is the international false prophet of the end times.

It could also be that the two horns of this beast are the two facets of false religion of the future: Christian and non-Christian. This is how he is able to encompass the whole earth with a false spiritual power. He includes everybody. (This is also portrayed in Revelation 17:15.)

2) Two Other Ways of Describing the Two Beasts

In Revelation 17:3, there is a woman called Mystery: Babylon the Great, the Mother of Harlots and of the Abominations of the Earth.[15] She is sitting on "a bright

---

[13]   Walvoord, op. cit., 205.

[14]   In Revelation 13:12, this beast is portrayed as being almost as powerful as the first beast. But he only causes everyone to worship the first beast.

[15]   This portrayal of this beast is found in The Holy Bible, New King James Version (Nashville: Thomas Nelson Publishers, 1992).

red beast covered with insulting names."[16] The two individuals in this verse will be seen to be as follows.

A. The Bright Red Beast Covered with Insulting Names

Because this beast is constantly blaspheming God, He has named him "Covered with Insulting Names."

Concerning this beast, Daniel 11:36 says, "Then the king shall do according to his own will: he shall exalt and magnify himself above every god, shall speak blasphemies against the God of gods, and shall prosper till the wrath has been accomplished." Since this is the case, the bright red beast is the Antichrist.

B. Mystery Babylon, also Known as a Harlot

While commenting on Revelation 17:1–12, the Wycliffe Bible Commentary says Babylon is

> some vast spiritual system that persecutes the saints of God, betraying that to which she was called. She enters into relations with the governments of this earth, and for a while rules them. I think the closest we can come to an identification ... is to understand this harlot as symbolic of a vast spiritual power arising at the end of the age which enters into a league with the world and

---

[16]   This portrayal of this beast is found in God's Word: Today's Bible Translation that Says What It Means (Orange Park, FL: God's Word to the Nations Bible Society, 1995).

> compromises with the worldly forces.
> Instead of being spiritually true she is
> spiritually false, and thus exercises an
> evil influence in the name of religion.[17]

Again, this is a description of the false prophet and the worldwide false religion over which he has control. The harlot rules for a while, but as we see in Revelation 17:16–17, she is destroyed by the ten horns. Then the red-colored beast rules alone.

3) Summary of the Two Beasts

We have seen the beast that comes out of the sea has been named "a bright red beast covered with insulting names" and is the Antichrist. And we have seen the beast that comes from the earth has been named "a harlot" and is the false prophet. We have also seen the Antichrist as a person who completely hates God and has the whole world under his control (Revelation 13:3). Likewise, we see the false prophet as having control of the one-world religious system during the tribulation period.

* * *

---

[17]   *The Wycliffe Bible Commentary,* edited by Charles F. Pfeiffer, Old Testament, and Everett F. Harrison, New Testament (Nashville: The Southwestern Company, 1962), 1,517.

The One-World Government, the One-World Church, and the Antichrist's Evil Empire

Two dreams are recorded in the Bible that explain what has been happening in history, and also what will be happening in the future. Nebuchadnezzar dreamed one dream and Daniel the other.

1) Nebuchadnezzar's Dream

Daniel 2:31–35 tells of Nebuchadnezzar's dream, and verses 36–45 give the interpretation of the dream. It is about a statue with a head of gold, chest and arms of silver, stomach and thighs of bronze, legs of iron, and feet partly of iron and partly of clay. He also dreamed that "the God of heaven will set up a kingdom which shall never be destroyed" in verses 44–45. This latter is the millennial kingdom of Jesus Christ (Zechariah 2:10–11, Revelation 20:2–5).

Daniel 2:38 says the head of gold is Nebuchadnezzar. So this part of the statue refers to ancient Babylon, of which Nebuchadnezzar was king. Verse 39 speaks of "another kingdom" arising after Nebuchadnezzar. This would be the silver part of the statue. Daniel 2:39 also speaks of a "third kingdom of bronze," and verse 40 describes the fourth kingdom as being "strong as iron."

But in Daniel 2:34–35, 44–45, the stone "cut out of the mountain without hands, [which] broke in pieces the iron, the bronze, the clay, the silver, and the gold" is speaking of Jesus Christ. And as we will see, it is also He who destroys the fourth beast of Daniel's dream in the future.

2) Daniel's Dream

Daniel's dream, told in Daniel 7:2–14, also had four beasts in it. Daniel 7:3 says, "And four great beasts came up from the sea, each different from the other." As you will notice, these beasts come out of the sea, as did the first beast of Revelation 13.

The first beast is found in Daniel 7:4: "The first was like a lion and had eagle's wings. I watched till its wings were plucked off; and it was lifted up from the earth, and made stand on two feet as a man, and a man's heart was given to it."

Stewart C. Easton, in his book *The Western Heritage: From the Earliest Times to the Present*, says that Babylon was like a lion in its dealings with Israel and the takeover of the world, [18] so this beast is ancient Babylon.

Henrietta C. Mears, in her book *What the Bible Is All About*, writes, "The first, or Babylon, was like a lion with eagle's wings."[19]

The second beast is found in Daniel 7:5: "And suddenly another beast, a second, like a bear. It was raised up on one side, and had three ribs in its mouth between its teeth. And they said thus unto it: 'arise, devour much flesh!'" That this beast is ancient Media-Persia is exemplified by the fact that the three ribs are Media, Babylon,[20] and Persia, which was formed

---

[18]   Stewart C. Easton, *The Western Heritage: From the Earliest Times to the Present*, 3rd edition (Austin, TX: Holt, Rinehart, & Winston Inc., 1970), 37–44.

[19]   Henrietta C. Mears, *What the Bible Is All About* (Ventura, CA: Gospel Light Publications, 1966), 267.

[20]   Babylon was in co-rulership with Media at this time in history (Easton, op. cit., 44, 53).

about this time by Cyrus, the Median king, after he conquered the other two.[21] Mears says that "Persia was the bear, the cruel animal who delights to kill for the sake of killing."[22] Easton says the Media-Persians were gruesome fighters who were always ready to go to war with their neighbors.[23]

The third beast is described in Daniel 7:6: "After this I looked, and there was another, like a leopard, which had on its back four wings of a bird. The beast also had four heads, and dominion was given to it." This beast is ancient Greece under the leadership of Alexander the Great, because it was given dominion over the whole known world at that time by his efforts.[24] Again I quote from Mears: "The third [beast] was a leopard or panther, a beast of prey. His four wings portray swiftness. Here we see the rapid marches of Alexander's army and his insatiable love of conquest."[25]

Also, the number four is mentioned twice in the biblical text, which denotes the division of ancient Greece into four parts.[26] (We find this also in Daniel 11:4.) These four sections each had a governor who corresponds to the four heads in our text.

The fourth and last beast is described in Daniel 7:7. It reads, "After this I saw in the night visions, and behold, a fourth beast, dreadful and terrible, exceedingly strong. It had huge iron teeth; it was devouring, braking in pieces, and trampling the residue with its feet. It was

---

[21]   Easton, op. cit., 44, 53.

[22]   Mears, op. cit., 267.

[23]   Easton, op. cit., 45.

[24]   Ibid., 101–104.

[25]   Mears, op. cit., 267.

[26]   Easton, op. cit., 101–104.

different from all the beasts that were before it, and it had ten horns."

This beast is certainly a terrible beast, because the text indicates it devoured and conquered everything in the world, and everything felt its iron rule.[27] Because of these things, this last beast is thought to be ancient Rome.

Mears only says that "The fourth beast was different from all the rest."[28]

One of the reasons this beast is so different is that it has toes of mixed iron and clay. This is portrayed in Daniel 2:40–43:

> And the fourth kingdom shall be strong as iron, inasmuch as iron breaks in pieces, and shatters everything; and like iron that crushes, that kingdom, will break in pieces and crush all the others.
>
> Whereas you saw the feet and toes, partly of potter's clay and partly of iron, the kingdom shall be divided; yet the strength of the iron shall be in it, just as you saw the iron mixed with ceramic clay.
>
> And as the toes of the feet were partly of iron and partly of clay, so the kingdom shall be partly strong, and partly fragile.

---

[27] Ibid., 118–162.
[28] Mears, op. cit., 268.

As you saw iron mixed with ceramic clay, they will mingle with the seed of men; but they will not adhere one to another, just as iron does not mix with clay.

The significance of this mixture of iron and clay that don't adhere to each other shows how the ancient Roman Empire was loosely held together by its armies. It also demonstrates how things have been since the time of the ancient Roman Empire. Many nations now make up the territory that once occupied that area.

3) What Is Learned from These Two Dreams

As can be seen, the two dreams parallel each other. They both have four earthly kingdoms: Babylon, Media-Persia, ancient Greece, and the ancient Roman Empire. And they both tell the story in which the last one is destroyed by Jesus Christ.

However, it is commonly thought the fourth beast turns into the revived Roman Empire of the future (i.e., "deadly wound was healed" in Revelation 13:3). This means it is revived as a one-world government, because it is an all-encompassing worldwide power.

This is found in Revelation 17:9–11:

Here is the mind which has wisdom: The seven heads are seven mountains on which the woman sits.

There are also seven kings. Five have fallen, one is, and the other has not yet come. And when he comes, he must continue a short time.

The beast that was, and is not, is himself also the eighth, and is of the seven, and is going to perdition.

But these mountains are not speaking of the city of Rome or even Jerusalem. Instead, they refer to seven imperialist world governments. Of this, John F. Walvoord writes,

The seven heads of the beast … are said to be symbolic of seven kings described in verse 10. Five of these are said to have fallen, one is in contemporary existence, that is, in John's lifetime, the seventh is yet to come and will be followed by another described as the eighth, which is the beast itself. In the Greek there is no word for "there," thus translated literally, the phrase is "and are seven kings." The seven heads are best explained as referring to seven kings who represent seven successive forms of the kingdom … [Scripture] does not say, "the seven heads are seven mountains, where the woman sits upon them" and there leave off; but [it] adds immediately, "and they are seven kings," or personified kingdoms. The mountains, then, are not piles of material rocks and earth at all, but royal or imperial powers.[29]

Revelation 17:9–11 speaks of the ancient Roman Empire as the sixth of all these encompassing world powers (i.e., "one is"). But the dreams only speak of four of them. The answer to this is that there were two world powers before Babylon. They are the Egyptian Empire and the Assyrian Empire.

In his book *Unleashing the Beast,* Perry Stone writes,

> Both past and future biblical prophecy is always linked to Israel and the Jewish people. Of the seven prophetic kings, John, when writing the book of Revelation, indicated that five had already fallen and no longer existed in John's time. These kingdoms began with the Egyptian Empire, which was the first major empire in the Bible to impact the Hebrew people for more than four hundred years (Gen. 15:13). These five kingdoms included: [the Egyptian Empire, the Assyrian Empire, the Babylonian Empire, the Medo-Persian Empire, and the Greek Empire.][30]

However, our text in Revelation 17:9–11 speaks not only the ancient Roman Empire as the one that was in

---

29   Walvoord, op. cit., 251–254.
30   Perry Stone, *Unleashing the Beast* (Lake Mary, FL: Front Line Charisma Media/Charisma House, 2009–2011), 21–22.

existence in John's day, but also of another one that has "not yet come" as the seventh beast. This speaks of the revival of the Roman Empire.

Leon Wood is another theologian who believes from the evidence presented in the book of Daniel that there will be a revival of the Roman Empire. While commenting on the fourth beast of Daniel 7:8, he writes,

> The correct view [of this] can only be that there will be a time still future when the Roman empire will be restored … a time when ten contemporary kings will rule, among whom another will arise, uprooting three in the process, and then move on to become the head of all … the new horn must symbolize another king, like the others, only emerging later, though while they still rule. Because the description of this ruler, given in this verse and later in verses twenty-four to twenty-six, corresponds to descriptions of the "beast" of Revelation 13:5–8 and 17:11–14, the two are correctly identified. The one so described is commonly and properly called the Antichrist, who will be Satan's counterfeit world ruler, trying to preempt the place of God's true world ruler, Jesus Christ, who will later establish His reign during the millennium.[31]

---

[31]   Leon Wood, *A Commentary on Daniel* (Grand Rapids, MI: Zondervan, 1973), 187–188.

Not only is the Roman Empire revived (which is a one-world government and the seventh "mountain" of Revelation 17:9–11), but a strong leader also emerges from it to become the ruler of the evil empire of the Antichrist (Revelation 13:4, 8; 17:11–12; Daniel 7:20–25). The strong leader's evil empire is the eighth "mountain" of Revelation 17:9–11. Who this is has not yet been revealed and won't be until after the rapture of the Church (2 Thessalonians 2:8).

* * *

"Now, that explains a lot of things that are going on!" I exclaimed. "Boano Schmidt must be the Antichrist spoken of in the Bible and is the first beast of Revelation 13."

"Yes! And St. Boniface must be the false prophet and the second beast of Revelation 13!" replied Jason.

"Wow!" Brad mused. "Things are falling right into place as Dad said the Bible predicted!"

"Are we going to go to church tomorrow?" asked Amanda.

"Do you think there will be anybody there?" I asked.

"Well, there might be because I know a lot of people my age who were skeptics like I was!" added Brad.

"Okay, let's go and see who is there," said Jason.

The next day, Brad drove his Jeep to church and met us there. He was happy to see that the authorities had gotten all the stalled cars out of the ditches. He wondered if angels had stopped the cars in just the right places, because there were hardly any accidents.

When we arrived, we went to our respective Sunday school rooms. Brad and Amanda found half of their youth group plus the youth pastor sitting in front of the fireplace in their special room. They all looked glum except the youth pastor, Nick Johnson.

"Good to see you, Bradley and Amanda," he said. "Have you two gone to get your invisible tattoo or ID mark yet?"

"Why should we do that?" Brad asked.

"You get an ID mark so you can work at your job and buy the things you need," he explained.

"Aren't you interested in the fact that so many people are missing, including my parents and siblings?"

"Oh, they were a bunch of nonconformists! We shouldn't worry about them!"

"You know you can't buy anything in any store unless you have it!" shouted Sarah, Brad's girlfriend. "Leaflets were dropped from helicopters last night, and it's all over the news! Furthermore, it's the headline in the Sunday paper today."

Jason and I went to where the youth were meeting, because Pastor Philip and his wife weren't at church. Pastor Phil had been giving the Sunday school lessons lately, which were about end-time events.

"We didn't want to listen to Deacon Smith talk about how great Boano was, so we came in here," I explained.

"Hi, Nick. I think Pastor Philip and Sue were raptured!" Jason added.

"Why are you coming in here talking about that? I'm in charge of this church now, and I don't want to hear anything about the rapture," said Nick.

"Well, it happened!" Amanda retorted.

"I say good riddance!" said Nick.

"Come on, guys! Let's go!" coaxed Jason.

"I'm coming, too," Sarah answered.

We all stopped at our house and ate some cold sandwiches.

"What's this about the rapture?" Sarah asked as we ate.

"It's when Jesus came Friday as a thief in the night to steal His own away, as it says He was going to do in 1 Thessalonians 5:2," explained Brad.

"So you and me and everyone who was not His own was left behind?" she asked.

"That's right. But we have accepted Jesus as our personal Savior since then."

"I've heard about that all my life, but I never thought I needed to."

Brad's phone rang just then. It was Ben, Brad's best friend.

"Nick called downtown to the police and said you guys were renegades and should be picked up," Ben proclaimed.

"What did they say?"

"They said they were booked up and would get to it as soon as possible. You better get the ID mark and fast, Brad!"

"Nick sure has the spirit of the Antichrist, doesn't he?" Brad asked.

"Whoa, I want to hear more about that! I'm coming over! Where are you?"

"I'm with Jason's family at their house. Do you know where it is?"

"Yes, I'll be right over!"

When Ben arrived, he ate a sandwich, and we filled him in on the rapture. We all then decided to go out to the farm.

"That driver's license check right outside of town sure was different," mused Ben. "What are they looking for?"

"Did you notice they were typing something into their tablets? I think they were recording us and checking with the huge computer in The Hague!" answered Brad.

"Hey, we learned about that in government class, didn't we?" asked Ben. "It's supposed to keep track of us in case anybody goes missing, especially children."

"Well, I think they are going to use it to find out who all the Christians are, too."

"They need to do that. I think they are going to be troublemakers for the new world community that Boano is trying to bring about. I also heard they are going to get their heads chopped off if they don't get the ID mark."

"Yeah, but then they will be instantly in heaven with Jesus!" exclaimed Brad.

"Not me! I don't want to get my head chopped off. In fact, I think I'll go back to town. Bye!"

"I'm going with you!" Sarah responded.

When Sarah and Ben got to the road at the end of the driveway, Ben peeled his tires and left some rubber. He had a hopped-up car he was very proud of.

"Wow, that shows their spiritual condition," said Amanda.

"I feel sorry for them," Brad explained. "They'll probably take the ID mark and end up in hell."

"What are we going to do?" I asked.

"We need to take your Jeep, Brad, and go to the cabin," said Jason. Our two families had invested in this property when the kids were younger. It was in a forest by a lake.

"That sounds like a good idea!" I exclaimed.

Brad and Jason put the car carrier that Brad had rigged up for his family's hunting excursions on top of the Jeep. Brad packed up some belongings, and we went to our place in town. We also packed as much as we could and put it in the car carrier. They added two huge tents and a cooking stove.

We took off for the cabin and encountered no resistance until we got to the state line. There we found a long line of cars awaiting inspection.

Brad quickly turned into a path leading into the forest, and we bumped along this path for about two miles until it ended. Brad then continued through the forest, dodging trees until we came to a stream in a small valley. There was a small, level meadow beside the stream.

It was about five o'clock in the evening, and Jason said, "Let's camp here for the night."

We began to set up camp with a tent for us ladies and another tent for Jason and Brad. I started to light the hibachi to cook the frozen hamburgers we had brought.

All of a sudden, a Jeep and a Hummer came over a knoll about a quarter mile away. After they approached, two officers with uniforms that had "OWC" on the front above the pocket got out of the Hummer. OWC probably stood for One-World Community. Their nametags were on the other side of their shirts, above the pockets. There were patches on their shoulders that resembled the logo I had seen so many times the last couple of days on the news.

The officer with sergeant stripes left the Hummer and yelled as he approached us, "You didn't stop on the interstate back there and tell us where you were going."

"We were tired and wanted to eat," answered Jason.

"Well, it looked like you were running from your duty to report in at all checkpoints!" the sergeant bellowed.

"Can we go back and do it now?" Jason asked.

"You better betcha! Judd here will stay with you as you break camp. Do everything he says!" The sergeant then brusquely turned around and got into the Jeep, where another guard was waiting behind the steering wheel.

Judd watched us as we packed everything up. He had his machine gun trained on us the entire time. We were then escorted back to the highway as he followed us in the Hummer.

We went to a small temporary office they had set up near the checkpoint. Judd then escorted us into the small structure.

"Why did you run into the woods when you were supposed to stop for inspection?" a lieutenant in the same kind of uniform asked in a sarcastic voice. "And why don't you have the ID mark?" he said as he scanned us with his iPhone.

"We're not going to get the ID mark!" Jason said.

"Oh, you're not?" the lieutenant asked even more sarcastically. "Well, we'll let the sheriff in Central City determine that. Take them to the bus," he quickly commanded Judd.

We were herded onto a small waiting bus where a teenage girl was sitting. She was handcuffed to the armrest of the seat—like Judd was doing to us.

Judd got off the bus, and I asked the girl, "What's your name?"

"Ashley," she answered.

"I'm Brad," our nephew said. "And this is my aunt Susan, uncle Jason, and cousin Amanda."

"Hi, Ashley," Amanda responded. "Do you know Jesus?"

"Oh, I should. But I don't think so. As you can see, I've been left behind. It was devastating when I couldn't find my parents!"

Ashley began crying, and I asked, "Would you like to accept Him now to make sure you will be going to heaven?"

"Oh, yes! I think I better!" Ashley prayed to let Jesus Christ come into her heart.

"Oh, it feels so good to get rid of all the guilt I've had since last Friday! Wow! Praise the Lord!" she exclaimed.

Judd came into the bus just then, pushing an older couple ahead of him. He heard us all praising the Lord and yelled, "You guys keep quiet. I'm tired of hearing all this religious talk" as he sneered at us.

"Praise the Lord!" the older man exclaimed. Judd slapped him across the cheek and quickly got off the bus. This was after handcuffing the older man and his wife to seats across the aisle from each other.

"Are you okay?" Jason asked the older man.

"Oh, yes! This is the first we've been assaulted. However, that guard did yank us around by our arms after we got out of the car. It was because we said we wouldn't get the ID mark!"

"Yeah, we've been treated rather badly too because of that," said Brad.

"We were told we are going to Central City," Brad explained to him. "I looked it up on my tablet, and it is a regional center with a guillotine!"

"Oh, my!" exclaimed the older lady. "It says in Revelation 20:4 that's what is going to happen! But we're ready to meet Jesus!"

At that moment, Judd came into the bus with another guard, but I don't think he heard the older lady. They were cruelly dragging a middle-aged couple by their handcuffs.

"Jerrod here is going to drive all you idiots to see the sheriff. He has been instructed to shoot anybody who utters a peep," Judd said loudly as he handcuffed the middle-aged guy to a seat.

"Yeah, not a peep!" Jerrod sneered, handcuffing the middle-aged lady to a seat across the aisle.

Jerrod silently drove us all to Central City. When we arrived, we were herded inside a huge church by Jerrod and two other guards with machine guns.

"Welcome to our little congregation," said a man in front of us with a microphone. He wore a badge below the OWC logo and what looked like a sheriff's uniform.

Just then, about ten of the fifty people across from us were escorted by one of the six guards at the side of the sanctuary. All the guards had machine guns. They went out a door to the side as our speaker continued his speech: "The people that just left are going to a court session in the fellowship hall. They will be given a chance to accept the mark of our beloved Boano by getting the tattoo. If they refuse this time, they will be executed tomorrow in the parking lot outside. Since you were interrupted in your travels, the judge has elected to give you this glorious second chance to take the ID mark. And if you do accept it, you will be given your vehicles back with an apology and sent on your way."

A half hour later, we were also escorted into the fellowship hall, where there was a judge's desk and chair high on a platform. There was no witness bench or jury box.

A stern-looking old judge took us in front of him one by one and asked, "Do you accept the conditions of our new economic efficiency by having a tattoo painlessly put on your forehead or on the back of your hand? By doing so, you will be obeying the law!"

I heard Jason refuse, and the judge proclaimed, "Death by the guillotine!" It was the same for me after Jason was escorted out to the parking lot where sixty or so others stood at attention in the hot sun.

After about ten minutes, Brad and Amanda, as well as everybody else who were on the bus ride from the state border, were outside. We were then escorted to small temporary jail houses on the property.

The next day, we were all executed.

EPILOGUE

Revelation 6:9 says, "When He opened the fifth seal, I saw under the altar the souls of those who had been slain for the word of God and for the testimony which they held." Since this verse of Scripture is in the context of the four horsemen of Revelation, these are those who were martyred in the great tribulation. They include Susan, Jason, Bradley, Amanda, and the other sixty people who were in the church sanctuary that day.

My plea is to accept Jesus now! You will not only experience a very rewarding Christian life on earth (John 10:9–10), but you will also be in heaven with Jesus Christ for all eternity (John 14:1–6).

Printed in the United States
By Bookmasters